DON'T MISS THE REST OF THE
SIXTH-GRADE ALIEN SERIES!

Sixth-Grade Alien

I Shrank My Teacher

Missing — One Brain!

Lunch Swap Disaster

Zombies of the Science Fair

Class Pet Catastrophe

Too Many Aliens

Snatched from Earth

There's an Alien in My Backpack

The Revolt of the Miniature Mutants

Coming Soon: *Aliens, Underwear, and Monsters*

Sixth-Gr... Ali...

The Revolt of
Miniature Mut

The Revolt
of the
Miniature
Mutants

By **BRUCE COVILLE**

Illustrated by Glen Mullaly

ALADDIN

NEW YORK   LONDON   TORONTO   SYDNEY   NEW DELHI

ALADDIN

An imprint of Simon & Schuster Children's Publishing Division

1230 Avenue of the Americas, New York, New York 10020

This Aladdin hardcover edition October 2021

Text copyright © 2001 by Bruce Coville

Illustrations copyright © 2021 by Glen Mullaly

Also available in an Aladdin paperback edition.

All rights reserved, including the right of reproduction in whole or in part in any form.

ALADDIN and related logo are registered trademarks of Simon & Schuster, Inc.

For information about special discounts for bulk purchases, please contact Simon & Schuster Special Sales at 1-866-506-1949 or business@simonandschuster.com.

The Simon & Schuster Speakers Bureau can bring authors to your live event. For more information or to book an event contact the Simon & Schuster Speakers Bureau at 1-866-248-3049 or visit our website at www.simonspeakers.com.

Designed by Tiara Iandiorio

The illustrations for this book were rendered in a mix of traditional and digital media.

The text of this book was set in Noyh Book.

Manufactured in the United States of America 0821 FFG

2 4 6 8 10 9 7 5 3 1

Library of Congress Control Number 2020952303

ISBN 9781534487345 (hc)

ISBN 9781534487338 (pbk)

ISBN 9781534487352 (ebook)

CONTENTS

FOR CHRISTINE BOUCHAREINE,
PLESKIT'S FAITHFUL FRIEND IN
FRANCE

Dear Class,
We just want you to
know it wasn't our fault!

Signed,
Your faithful hamsters
Ronald Roundbutt
Hubert Hugecheeks

P.S. Please notice—
Doris didn't sign this!

P.P.S. Ronald wrote it.

CHAPTER 1

[PLESKIT]
HAMSTER HORROR

Sometimes I wake up screaming. Usually it's because I've eaten too much *febril gnurxis* just before bedtime. But sometimes . . . sometimes it's because I see the furious, furry face of a hamster in my dreams.

It's been a rough year.

First the Fatherly One dragged me here to Earth. As if being so far from Hevi-Hevi (my beloved home planet) weren't bad enough, I have had the usual problems of fitting into a new school. These were made more difficult by the fact that I am the only student in my class who is purple and has a *sphen-gnut-ksher* growing out of his head.

Even moving might not have been so bad, if we

hadn't also had to deal with several attempts to sabotage the Fatherly One's mission. It was only recently that we discovered the reason for these attempts — a previously undiscovered Grand *Urpelli* so close to Earth that it falls within the Fatherly One's trading franchise.

Urpelli are the shortcuts through space that make interstellar travel possible. Still, it can be a long way between *urpelli*, which is why a Grand *Urpelli* is so important. It links all the others into a sort of galaxy-wide Internet. Until the one near Earth was discovered, everyone thought there was only one Grand *Urpelli* in the entire galaxy.

Whoever controls this second Grand *Urpelli* (which is now being called "Gurp Two" for short) will become one of the richest beings in the galaxy.

It is still hard for me to imagine that. I mean, we have always had a good life. But if the Fatherly One can hold on to his claim, we will have more money than . . . well, than just about anyone!

It's a little scary.

Anyway, given the value of Gurp Two, it's no surprise that others want to get their hands on it. What *has* been a surprise is how badly they will behave to do so.

The Revolt of the Miniature Mutants

The greatest enemy we have faced in all this was Mikta-makta-mookta, the Fatherly One's traitorous former secretary. She was never *really* a secretary, of course; just an evil genius disguising herself as one.

And since Mikta-makta-mookta looks a good deal like a five-foot-tall version of the Earthly creature called a hamster (or, to put it another way, a hamster looks the way Mikta-makta-mookta would if you shrank her), it should be no surprise that I have a genuine fear of hamsters, as cute and cuddly as they may seem to most people.

This was exactly what my demented and evil classmate, Jordan Lynch, was counting on when he began using them to torment me.

"Demented" and "evil" are strong words to apply to a fellow being, of course. In my opinion Jordan has earned them. He is the kind of person who . . . well, imagine that you and Jordan had just crawled across the desert and were dying of thirst, and you came to a place where there were two glasses of water. If Jordan got there first, he would save one of them for you — but he'd spit in it before he handed it to you, just to see if you'd still drink it.

Wakkam Akkim, the Fatherly One's spiritual massage-master, says that Jordan must be a troubled soul,

3

seeking answers for questions he cannot even name.

Wakkam Akkim would say that.

Tim Tompkins, my best friend here on Earth, has a simpler explanation. He says that the universe has a certain amount of evil, and sometimes it just comes together in one place and erupts, like a pimple.

"That's Jordan," says Tim. "A hot red pimple of evil festering on the face of the universe."

Certainly that seems like a reasonable description of Jordan the day he slipped the cutest and cuddliest of the class hamsters — Doris the Delightful, to be precise — into my lunchbox.

I often bring my lunch to school, for two reasons. First, Shhh-foop, our Queen of the Kitchen, makes splendid food. Second, I have not been able to get used to the food served in the cafeteria.

"Don't worry about it, Pleskit," says Tim when we discuss this problem. "No reasonable being could ever get used to these mysterious substances."

Tim also told me he used to believe that the school imported the food from outer space. But I told him that I knew of no other planet where people ate this kind of *koobtiuk*. In fact, I fear the phenomenon of cafeteria

4

The Revolt of the Miniature Mutants

food offers uncomfortable proof of the Fatherly One's claim that the people in our host country are secretly at war with their children.

(Even so, I have to admit that I have developed a deep fondness for ketchup, which is my favorite dessert.)

Anyway, on this particular day I had opened my lunchbox and was about to take out my *squambul* pod when Brad Kent called my name.

I should have known better than to answer.

Brad follows Jordan around like a *gerton-farkus*, so I should have guessed that he was simply doing Jordan's dirty work. But, like fools, Tim and I turned in his direction.

"What is it, Brad?" I asked.

He smiled and waved. "Just wanted to see if you remembered my name!"

I sighed and turned back to talk to Tim. At the same time I reached into my lunchbox.

Instead of my *squambul* pod, I grabbed something furry—something that was wriggling.

I looked at my hand.

I began to scream.

5

CHAPTER 2

[TIM]
BAG O' TRICKS

When Pleskit started to scream, I thought at first he had been attacked or had felt a sudden need to perform some alien ritual.

Then I realized it was just because he was holding a hamster.

His screams alerted Robert McNally, his official bodyguard (and my unofficial hero). Within seconds McNally was bounding across the cafeteria to see what was the matter.

Now, if McNally thinks Pleskit is in danger, he will not hesitate to do what is necessary. Which is why, when some kids got in his way, he simply jumped onto

The Revolt of the Miniature Mutants

one of the tables — squashing numerous lunches in the process.

Some people seem to believe that if you cannot eat a piece of food, the only thing to do with it is throw it. Within seconds the air was filled with two things: the words "Food fight," and people's lunches.

Someone with a butterfly net could have fed a lot of starving children with what they snatched out of the air in that cafeteria.

Meanwhile, Pleskit was still screaming. He stopped when McNally got to our table and grabbed the hamster — it turned out to be Doris — out of his hand.

McNally looked at the squirming ball of fur and shook his head. "Pleskit," he said, "you have *got* to get over this hamster thing."

Pleskit's answer was cut off by Principal Grand, who came storming into the cafeteria and bellowed, "Stop that this instant!"

Everyone stopped. You could hear food splatting to the floor all around us.

"All right," said Mr. Grand. "What is going on here?"

Pleskit was still too discombobulated to speak. So I explained the situation.

Mr. Grand remained very not happy. "Jordan was completely out of line," he said. "However, you really need to stop being so reactive, Pleskit. It was just a hamster, for heaven's sake!" He turned to McNally. "As for you, sir . . . I would deeply appreciate it if you could refrain from walking on the tables and trampling pupils' lunches."

McNally nodded. "Request noted and logged, sir."

What he didn't say—but what I knew he was thinking—was that if he thought Pleskit was in danger, he'd be back on top of those tables in a heartbeat.

I'd like to be like McNally when I grow up.

When I got home from school that night, my mother was sitting at the dining room table, reading the *National Scoop,* one of those skeezy newspapers they sell at supermarket checkout counters. I used to think the *Scoop* was pretty cool, because it had stories like PRESIDENT'S WIFE GIVES BIRTH TO TWO-HEADED BULLDOG and things like that. Then I figured out they were just making it all up, which really bugged me.

What bugs me even more is that the paper is fiercely

The Revolt of the Miniature Mutants

anti-alien. It's always trying to whip up some scandal about Meenom's peaceful trade mission.

"Mom!" I cried in disgust. "Why are you reading that thing?"

"It falls in the category of 'know your enemy,'" she said. "They're after Pleskit's Fatherly One again."

She put the paper down, acting as if she were handling a dirty diaper. Now I could see the full front of it. The headline, in huge letters, shrieked ALIEN AMBASSADOR'S LOVE SCANDAL! Under the headline was a picture of Ambassador Meenom standing next to Ms. Buttsman, the embassy's Earthling protocol officer.

"They have *got* to be kidding," I said. "The Butt is about as lovable as a tarantula."

My mother used to object to my calling Ms. Buttsman "The Butt," until she actually met her. Now she does it too.

"Unfortunately, they're serious," she said. "What's even worse, a lot of idiots are going to take it as fact just because they read it."

I sighed. "Can we move to another planet?"

"Have you finished your homework?" she replied.

This was her way of telling me to drop it.

Bruce Coville

I trudged into my room.

Rather than settling down to my homework, I took a cloth bag out of my dresser. It held tricks and puzzles that Beebo Frimbat, a mischief-making little alien from the planet Roogbat, had left with me as a sort of thank-you for putting up with him. I had two other things that belonged to Beebo: his diary, a tiny book that I couldn't read (since it was written in an alien language); and the body suit he had worn to disguise himself as an Earthling.

The body suit stands in my closet, looking for all the world as if it were a real human boy who had somehow just . . . stopped. I keep the closet door closed at night because the suit kind of weirds me out.

The tricks and puzzles would have been totally baffling, except Beebo had very kindly taken the time to translate the names and directions for me.

The puzzles were tough. I hadn't managed to solve any, though I was getting close on the Sircassian Belly Knot. Right then I was more interested in the tricks. They included such gems as the Infinite Voice Generator (guaranteed to give you a new voice every time you use it), Never-Fail Hair Tonic (guaranteed to

The Revolt of the Miniature Mutants

grow thick, luxuriant hair wherever it is applied, hair not to last more than seventy-two hours), and, the one that I found most intriguing, the Fabulous Fizzy Fart Bomb. (A thousand laughs! Highly embarrassing!

Guaranteed completely safe for all organic creatures!)

Surely one of these would be appropriate to use on the kind of kid who would sneak a hamster into an alien's lunchbox.

I called my friend Rafaella Martinez.

CHAPTER 3

[PLESKIT]
ADVICE FROM THE
WAKKAM

When McNally and I returned to the embassy that afternoon, we went to the kitchen for a snack, as usual. Shhh-foop was sliding around, waving the tentacles that grow from the top of her head and gurgling happily to herself as she gathered the food.

Barvgis, the Fatherly One's assistant, was there. This was not surprising; he is often in the kitchen, increasing his roundness. I was, however, surprised to see the Fatherly One, who has not been present much lately, despite his promises to spend more time with me. I could understand his absences—the pressures

13

involved in trying to become the richest person in the galaxy are considerable.

Even so, I missed him.

He was looking particularly gloomy at the moment.

"What is the matter, O beloved parental unit?" I asked.

He emitted the smell of disgust. "My enemies have started another negative publicity campaign. Now they are claiming that I am obsessed with Earth women! They have even linked me romantically with . . . Ms. Buttsman!"

"This seems to be a particular fear of Earthlings," said Barvgis.

"You mean Ms. Buttsman terrorizes the whole planet?" I asked.

Barvgis chuckled. "No, no. But for some reason, Earthlings seem to always believe that everyone wants their women. Hard to understand why, when they're all so skinny!"

Barvgis does not believe in skinniness. In fact, he is the roundest being I have ever met. Also the slimiest. This makes it confusing to me when Earthlings use the word "slimeball" as an insult, since Barvgis is probably one of the nicest beings in the galaxy.

The Revolt of the Miniature Mutants

"How went *your* day?" asked the Fatherly One, turning to me.

"Another minor catastrophe," I said gloomily.

Barvgis dug his hand into the bowl of squirmers sitting in front of him. "Why should this day be different from any other?" he asked, just before he tossed the little creatures into his mouth. The sound of their tiny screams was cut off by him clamping his lips shut.

"Perhaps Pleskit should seek counsel and advice from the esteemed *wakkam*," sang Shhh-foop as she placed a bowl of *febril gnurxis* in front of me. "Some coffee for the heroic Just McNally?" she warbled.

McNally glanced at his watch. "Uh, not today, Shhh-foop," he said, doing a heroic job of pretending to be distressed that he wouldn't have time for a cup of coffee. "I have to go do some reports."

McNally is a brave man, but he does seem to have become terrified by Shhh-foop's repeated failures to properly brew this Earthly beverage.

As he left the room, I turned my mind to Shhh-foop's suggestion that I ask advice of *Wakkam* Akkim. The *wakkam* does give good advice. The only problem is, it is not always easy to understand. I decided I would try anyway. So after my snack I went to the wall and burped a request to the embassy tracking system.

It informed me that the *wakkam* was in her room.

I took the elevator up—she lives on an upper floor, for the sake of privacy—then went to her door. When I signaled that I wanted to enter, the door slid right open. (I was surprised; I had expected to hear her voice, asking what I wanted.)

The room was dark. Strange blue smoke drifted through the air, rich with the scent of other worlds.

"*Wakkam* Akkim?" I called softly.

"Here," she replied, her voice low and gentle. "In the next chamber."

I was pleased. The second chamber is her sacred "inner sanctum," and I had not yet seen it.

The room was draped with dark fabrics. Brightly colored pillows were strewn about the floor. Soft *bezooti* music played. The *wakkam* sat cross-legged on a feathery stool, her hands palms-up on her knees, her eyes closed.

I stood without speaking. She seemed to be deep in thought, and after a little while I began to wonder if I should go. But after another few moments, without even opening her eyes, she said, "How can I help you, Pleskit?"

I explained some of the trouble I was having in school.

"Ah," she said, "I see." (Which is sort of an odd thing to say when you have your eyes closed.) "Wait a minute, please."

She mumbled and murmured to herself, then said

in an eerie voice, "He who would conquer his fear must face it. He who would love his fear must nurture it."

I stared at her in puzzlement. "What's that supposed to mean?"

She said nothing. Sometimes she does that—just makes a weird pronouncement, then goes all quiet. This basically means you're supposed to figure it out for yourself.

If you manage to do that, things usually work out well.

Notice, I said "if."

I thought about her words.

I had a fear of hamsters. Specifically, I was having a problem with Ronald, Doris, and Hubert. Did I want to conquer that fear, or love it?

Well, I didn't actually want to conquer the hamsters, who were really just cute little rodents after all.

Did that mean I should try to learn to love them? The *wakkam* had said the way to do that was to nourish them.

Well, if that was the prescription, I was going to do it all the way. I would nourish them as they had never been nourished before. This problem had to be solved!

I went straight to the embassy's laboratory and began working on a special nutritional supplement

The Revolt of the Miniature Mutants

that would give those hamsters energy, strength, and vitality. I started by hooking into the master computer. I spent hours gathering data on nurturing small Earthly animals. Then I gathered chemicals, some of them quite rare. Finally I threw myself into the Hevi-Hevian creative trance state.

I cannot actually tell you what went on while I was in this state, since the creative trance is a hyper-focused blur of activity.

All I can say is that when I was done, the lab was a mess. But in my hand I had . . . hamster mega-vitamins!

CHAPTER 4

[T I M]
FFFB

The day after the hamster-in-the-lunchbox incident, two things happened.

First, I passed the FFFB (that's short for "Fabulous Fizzy Fart Bomb") to Rafaella, who was going to try to give it to Jordan.

The FFFB looked like a piece of candy. I knew that Jordan sometimes hung around with Misty Longacres and some of the other girls, including Rafaella, and that when he did, he always mooched candy off them.

Second — and this happened at about ten thirty — I noticed Pleskit standing at the hamster cage, feeding something to Doris, Ronald, and Hubert.

The Revolt of the Miniature Mutants

This was a totally un-Pleskit-like thing to do, since his usual response to the sight of the little furballs was to shudder. So when we went outside for our run-around later that morning (Ms. Weintraub had decided we were too old for "playtime" and "recess," and had started referring to our time outdoors as "the run-around"), I pulled Pleskit aside and said, "Okay, what's the deal?"

"You want to make a deal?" he asked, looking all excited.

Sometimes I forget that he comes from a planet of Traders, where "deal" is the most exciting word in the dictionary.

"Not that kind of deal," I said. "I just want to know what's going on with you and the hamsters."

He instantly got all wide-eyed and innocent. "Nothing," he said.

"Then what were you doing over at their cage this morning?"

"Nothing," he said again. He tried to sound casual, but I knew he was fibbing, because his *sphen-gnut-ksher* emitted a slightly oily smell. Even though I haven't really begun to understand how to communicate in Hevi-Hevian, which uses smells as well as words (according to Pleskit, Earthly noses just aren't sensitive enough for it), I knew *that* smell. It was the odor he makes if he's not careful when he stretches the truth.

He saw me wrinkle my nose, and realized at once that he had given himself away.

"I liked it better before you knew how to interpret odors," he said. "However, since you have figured out that I am indeed up to something —"

Then he explained to me how he was giving the hamsters vitamins as a way to face his fear.

"Sounds pretty New Age to me," I said, pronouncing "New Age" so that it rhymed with "sewage," the way my mother always does. "And what's the big secret about, anyway?"

"I am keeping this secret not because there is anything wrong with what I am doing — it's just nutrition, after all — but because my reasons for taking the action are very private. Making a big deal out of it would be like — well, like having therapy in public."

"Okay," I said. "Your secret is safe with me."

As we were coming in from outside, Rafaella gave me the thumbs-up sign.

The Revolt of the Miniature Mutants

I could hardly keep from laughing out loud.

Jordan had swallowed the fart bomb.

When we got back from art class that afternoon, Ms. Weintraub called us to order and said, "Listen, everyone, I've got some good news! After considerable hesitation, Mr. Grand has approved the annual sixth-grade sleepover."

"Why was he hesitating?" asked Michael Wu.

Before Ms. Weintraub could answer, Jordan farted. It was a small but unmistakable fizzy splurt of a sound. He looked startled for just a second, then immediately arranged his face into the classic *Who did that?* look.

I had a hard time controlling my laughter. And I didn't dare look at Rafaella, because I knew I wouldn't have a chance of controlling myself.

Ms. Weintraub wrinkled her brow, then said, "Let's just say that it's been a difficult year, Michael."

Jordan snorted. "That's like saying an atomic bomb makes a big noise."

Then he made an explosion himself. It wasn't quite atomic-bomb level. But it was big enough so that everyone knew it had come from him.

Bursts of laughter from around the room were stifled by a glare from Ms. Weintraub. "I have some additional good news," she said, hurrying on. "Our friend Mr. Canterfield has agreed to come back to spend the evening with us."

By "Mr. Canterfield" she meant Percy the Mad Poet, of course. Percy's been coming in to teach a unit on poetry writing every year since we were in second grade. You might not think having a poet come visit us for the sleepover would be any big deal, but Percy is incredibly cool—something he had demonstrated beyond doubt when he'd helped Pleskit the time he ran away to keep his Veeblax from getting fried.

"Mr. Canterfield is going to lead a poetry jam that night," said Ms. Weintraub. "So we'll have to start working on our poems pretty soon."

Splort spluh splort splort! went Jordan.

"Very poetic, in a Hevi-Hevian sense," said Pleskit.

The class exploded in laughter.

Jordan just kept exploding, a veritable symphony of gas in an astonishing variety of tones and volumes.

Finally Ms. Weintraub said gently, "I think you'd better go see the nurse, Jordan."

The Revolt of the Miniature Mutants

Jordan emitted a sound like a string of firecrackers.

Ms. Weintraub burst out laughing.

Jordan, blushing furiously, raced out of the room.

We could hear him farting all the way down the hall.

While the other kids were still laughing, I happened to glance over at the counter where the hamster cage sat.

My laughter died on my lips.

Hubert, Doris, and Ronald were sitting up and watching us — watching intently, their heads cocked to one side, as if they were listening.

Almost as if they were trying to understand.

They couldn't really be paying attention to us.

Could they?

CHAPTER 5

[PLESKIT]
MUTANTS

At first the hamsters seemed to thrive under my vitamin treatment. Their beady little eyes glistened and flashed, their coats grew thick and glossy, and they spent more time than ever scuttling around in their tubes and running on their exercise wheel.

However, I noticed that they were also starting to get bigger. You might not have realized this if you were not keeping a close eye on them, but it was definitely happening.

I wasn't sure this was such a good thing. I mean, a hamster is supposed to be a certain size. As Tim says, "If they get too big, they start to look like guinea pigs."

The Revolt of the Miniature Mutants

And then, about a week after I had started giving them the vitamins, something very disturbing happened. Misty Longacres had gone over to the cage, as she often does. Suddenly she yelped and jumped backward.

"Did you hear that?" she cried.

"What?" asked several people.

"Doris growled at me!"

Everyone clustered around the cage—though not too close.

The hamsters, who had been sitting up, dropped to all fours and stared at us stupidly.

I had a terrible feeling that they were faking.

"What did you do to Doris, Misty?" asked Jordan. "Show her your face?"

"I didn't do anything!" said Misty, her eyes still wide with shock. "I was just going to pick her up."

"Something weird is going on with those hamsters," said Chris Mellblom darkly. "I've been noticing it for a few days now."

"You're not kidding," said Rafaella. "Hamsters definitely don't growl."

"Well, hamsters *can* be vicious," said Larrabe Hicks.

Rafaella rolled her eyes. "What are you talking about, Larrabe? They're sweet little fuzzballs."

"Are you forgetting the time I brought in my woodchuck and Hubert went psycho?" asked Larrabe. "And that's not all."

"What do you mean?" asked Chris.

Larrabe lowered his voice and looked around as if he were telling a ghost story at a campfire. "My mother had a hamster when she was a kid. She had a little mouse, too. She thought they were both sweet, so she put them in the cage together. The next day . . . the mouse was dead!"

"So how do you know it was the hamster's fault?" asked Michael Wu. "Couldn't the mouse just have died?"

"Its head was gone," said Larrabe.

"*Eeeuw!*" cried Misty. "That's disgusting, Larrabe! Don't tell stories like that!"

"Well, I'm not making it up, you know," said Larrabe, sounding hurt.

"Hey, these guys don't even *look* the same," said Michael suddenly. "Aren't their legs longer than they used to be?"

Everyone clustered closer to the cage again.

The Revolt of the Miniature Mutants

"They are!" said Misty. "What the heck is going on here?"

"I don't know what's going on," said Jordan. "But I do know Pleskit's been spending a lot of time by their cage lately. What are you doing, Ples — giving them alien radiation treatments?"

"Good one, Jordan!" said Brad Kent.

No one else laughed.

"All right!" said Ms. Weintraub sharply. "Back to your seats, all of you! The hamsters are fine. You're probably making them nervous with too much attention."

But from the look on her face, I wasn't sure she totally believed this herself.

I sat down, feeling tremendous guilt. Jordan had come uncomfortably close to the truth. Was my vitamin treatment really mutating the hamsters? Could it actually be making them vicious?

I thought about the hamsters all that evening. Well, most of the evening. I was interrupted by a visit from the Fatherly One — a very unusual circumstance, since he normally summons me to his office when he wants to see me.

29

"Greetings, revered parental unit," I said.

"Greetings, beloved but often neglected child-ling," he replied.

"It's true that I am often neglected," I said. "However, I know that it is not easy to become the richest being in the galaxy."

I did not mean this remark to be sarcastic, but the Fatherly One seemed to take it that way. "You are developing a sharp tongue," he said.

I belched an apology.

The Fatherly One nodded. "The reason I came to see you," he said, "is that your instructor, Ms. Weintraub, has contacted me regarding the overnight you are having at your school."

"She contacted you?" I asked in surprise. "Why?"

"First, she wanted to be sure it was all right for you to attend. Second, she wanted to know if *I* would come as well, perhaps to tell a story at the midnight gathering." He looked at me carefully. "How would you feel about that?"

I thought for a second. I had been somewhat embarrassed the first time the Fatherly One had come to our school, but that was mostly because Jordan had

The Revolt of the Miniature Mutants

made me feel that way. I had since learned that the other kids thought the Fatherly One was "cool."

"I think it would be wonderful," I said.

The Fatherly One smiled. "I am glad you like the idea. I will call Ms. Weintraub and accept her invitation."

He turned to leave the room.

"Fatherly One?" I said as he reached the door.

He turned. "Yes, my childling?"

"Thank you."

He smiled. "You are welcome, youngling."

That was my pleasant surprise for the week. The next day in school I got an unpleasant surprise. The hamsters were becoming more aggressive than ever. In fact, they kept standing on their hind legs and shaking their paws at us.

I was plunged into guilt — and also confusion. It was not as if I had been feeding them meat or anything.

But whatever was going on, it was clearly time to stop the mega-vitamin treatment.

So I did.

Now here's the really scary thing: even though I

stopped giving the hamsters vitamins, they continued changing. On Monday of the following week, we saw something truly strange. The hamsters began moving some of the stuff in their cage around, stacking pieces of wood on top of one another.

"It's almost as if they were trying to . . . to build something!" said Rafaella in awe.

I stared at the cage in dismay. What had I created?

CHAPTER 6

[T I M]
A CHAT WITH
MS. WEINTRAUB

The day we saw the hamsters stacking the blocks in their cage, I stayed after school to get a closer look at them. I wanted to see if I could figure out what was going on.

All right, that's not entirely true. At that time I was staying after school *every* day, because I was still making up the work I had missed while Pleskit and I had been off on Billa Kindikan, trying to save the galaxy.

Okay, okay—what we were really trying to do was *survive*. We just happened to save galactic civilization from collapse in the process. The end result was the same, and I still think a kid who prevented a galaxywide catastrophe shouldn't end up on permanent detention just because he missed a little work while he was off doing it.

My mother and Ms. Weintraub disagree.

So I was still making up work. Pleskit had to make it up too, of course, but with his mighty brain it only took a couple of days, which was annoying.

The only good thing I can say about the detention situation was that it came in useful whenever I needed to check out something in the classroom in private.

Anyway, there I was, sitting at my desk, as usual. But on this particular day, instead of just giving me some work to start on, Ms. Weintraub came and sat down at the desk next to mine. She looked at me for a minute, then said, "What are we going to do about you and Jordan, Tim?"

I had a nervous feeling that this was about the Fabulous Fizzy Fart Bomb. But since it had never been proved that Jordan's intestinal eruption had been anything other than a spectacular case of indigestion, I wasn't going to say anything about that unless I had to.

"Why don't you ask Jordan?" I said. "He's the one who's always picking on me."

The Revolt of the Miniature Mutants

She nodded. "I know. I've been watching it all year. And I *have* spoken to him, more than once. I've even spoken to his parents about it. Nothing seems to do any good." She leaned a little closer. "I just don't want to see things escalate," she said, her voice low but intense.

Yep, this was about the FFFB.

I just shrugged. What did she want me to do? Be a doormat for him?

Actually, that was just one of the questions I would have liked to ask Ms. Weintraub right then. I had several others on my mind — primarily: What's the deal with you and McNally?

And: Do you have any advice for me about what's going on with me and Rafaella? (I mean, what is *that* all about, anyway?)

That last thing was the topic I was most interested in. But I didn't say anything because I was too embarrassed to talk about it.

My mother (who watches *Oprah* too much, if you ask me) is always going on about how men are afraid to reveal their true feelings.

She should try being a guy for a while.

Anyway, the talk with Ms. Weintraub did give me

some second thoughts about having used the Fabulous Fizzy Fart Bomb on Jordan. Well, it was too late now; it was already done. And, to be truthful, I still couldn't really say that I regretted it—though I knew I'd sure regret it if he could ever prove it was actually my fault. (I'm sure he suspected it was, but he had no proof.)

"Okay, Tim," said Ms. Weintraub. "I just wanted to say something to you about all that. Now get started on these math sheets while I go take care of a couple of things."

Normally that would have really annoyed me. I mean, why keep me after if she's just going to give me stuff I could do at home? But in this case I didn't mind, because it gave me a perfect opportunity to take a closer look at the hamsters.

I didn't go right over and watch—at least, not at first. I had a feeling they were getting so smart that if they thought I was watching them, they would just play dumb. So I sat at my desk, pretending to work. But I was really watching the hamsters out of the corner of my eye.

The first weird thing I saw was Ronald running on the exercise wheel. That wouldn't normally have been all that strange; the hamsters spend a lot of time on that wheel. But usually they do it on all fours. Ronald was standing on his hind legs, pumping his arms and running like a mini-jogger!

Suddenly Doris stood up and waved her short little arms in what looked like a signal.

Hubert stood up too.

Ronald jumped off the wheel. Then the three of them lined up side by side and started to march across the cage. They looked as if they were doing military maneuvers!

I was so startled that I gasped.

Immediately all three of them dropped back down and began sniffing around as if they were looking for pellets.

I got up and went over to the cage. I stood there for a while, staring at them.

They just looked up at me, blinking stupidly.

Then I noticed something on the counter beside the cage, something that sent a chill skittering down my spine.

I picked it up and slipped it into my pocket, planning to show it to Pleskit as soon as I could.

Things were clearly getting out of hand.

CHAPTER 7

[T I M]
RAFAELLA

I intended to head straight for the embassy as soon as Ms. Weintraub let me go, but when I got to the bike rack behind the school, I found Rafaella waiting for me.

"Hey, Tim," she said. "I want to talk to you."

I hadn't been expecting this, but I didn't mind it either. Ever since Pleskit and I had come back from Billa Kindikan, Rafaella had been sort of paying attention to me, which I sort of liked. She's cooler than I gave her credit for. It turns out, for example, that she actually likes *Tarbox Moon Warriors*, my favorite old show. Not to mention the fact that she saved me from

The Revolt of the Miniature Mutants

getting creamed by Jordan when Beebo was causing so much trouble.

Or that she was willing to give the FFFB to Jordan.

I kind of think she's okay.

Also, she's pretty cute. The thing is, whenever I think about that, I feel a little guilty about Linnsy, my former upstairs neighbor who is now off somewhere exploring the galaxy with her symbiotic partner, Bur. I can't figure out why I should feel guilty. Linnsy was a pretty good friend, but she was more likely to want to go out with a can of sardines than she was to consider me boyfriend material.

I doubt I'll ever figure this stuff out.

Anyway, I didn't mind being delayed as much as I normally would have.

"What do you want to talk about?" I asked.

"Hamsters." She narrowed her eyes. "There's definitely something weird going on with our class pets. So — what do you know about it?"

I hesitated. Pleskit had told me about the hamster vitamins in confidence. On the other hand, Rafaella had come to the embassy with me at the climax of the Beebo problem, and she had kept her mouth shut about that whole mess. So she had proved she could be trusted. In a way, she was starting to fill the hole in my life that had opened up when Linnsy had gone away.

My hesitation confirmed Rafaella's suspicion that I knew something about what was going on.

"Come on, Tim," she said. "Spill."

I almost jumped at those words. Linnsy used to say the exact same thing when she wanted information from me. But she would give it as a command. With Rafaella, it was more of a request—her voice softer, her dark brown eyes doing half the asking.

I felt all funny inside.

And I talked.

This makes me think I would probably not make a very good spy, or do well on one of those missions where you have to keep your mouth shut because the fate of the world depends on your silence.

"Pleskit's been feeding them some alien megavitamins," I said.

Rafaella nodded. "I thought it must be something like that." She paused, then added, "Most people wouldn't guess it, but I probably know more about hamsters than anyone else in the class."

The Revolt of the Miniature Mutants

"You do?" I said in surprise.

"I *love* hamsters. I raised them for three years, starting when I was in first grade." She got a funny look on her face, then said, "Don't tell anyone, but when I was little, my mother used to raise these Russian dwarf hamsters." She looked around to make sure there was no one near us, then got a weird smile on her face. "The babies were so cute, I used to put them in my mouth and carry them around!"

"*Eeeuw!*" I cried. "Didn't they suffocate or anything?"

She looked at me as if I were some kind of moron. "I didn't leave them in there that long! And I'd open my mouth to let air in. I just wanted them close to me."

"Did you ever swallow one?"

She rolled her eyes. "Don't be such a dork, Tim."

"I can't help it. It seems to be my natural state."

She smiled, which did something funny to my insides. "There's more hope for you than you realize, Tim. Come on, we'd better go talk to Pleskit about this hamster thing."

Now this created an interesting situation. I had already been planning to do just that. But I hadn't been planning on taking Rafaella with me.

What would Pleskit think if we showed up together? What would Rafaella think if I told her she couldn't go? And why does life have to be so stinking complicated? (My mother assures me it only gets more so as time goes on. This fact, let me tell you, does not thrill me.)

Finally I said, "Sure, let's go."

Do you think I made a bold decision?

Hah!

I didn't make a choice at all. It was just that, since Rafaella was the one I was talking to right then, it was easier to take her along, and worry about what Pleskit might think later.

Plus I had this thing in my pocket that I *had* to show him, and I hoped that when I did, he would be so concerned about it that he would forget any questions he might have about me showing up with Rafaella.

They let us into the embassy with no problem.

Pleskit seemed surprised, but not upset, to see that Rafaella was with me.

Shhh-foop provided a weird but tasty snack called Gadroobian tongue-ticklers. Then the three of us went into a private room to talk.

The Revolt of the Miniature Mutants

"Rafaella raises hamsters," I said, partly by way of explaining why she was with me.

"Well, not anymore," she said.

"But I thought you said —"

"I *used* to raise hamsters. Then I got interested in snakes instead."

"You raise snakes?" I yelped.

"Snakes and lizards."

"How come I never knew this?"

She made a little snort, then said, "There's a lot about me you don't know, Tim."

Well, that was obviously true.

Pleskit intervened. "You said you had something to show me."

"Yeah. I found *this* next to the hamster cage this afternoon. "

I reached into my pocket and took out the thing I had picked up off the counter.

"Uh-oh," Pleskit said.

CHAPTER 8

[PLESKIT]
THE TRAP

Lying in the palm of Tim's hand was a tiny glove, just the right size for a hamster.

"Are you sure that's not just a doll's glove that someone left there by accident?" said Rafaella.

Tim looked at her in surprise. "None of the girls in our class play with dolls, do they?"

Rafaella shook her head. "Tim, don't even try to imagine you know anything about the lives of women."

"We can check easily enough," I said. "Let's do a molecular analysis."

"That's one reason I like coming here," said Tim.

The Revolt of the Miniature Mutants

"Some problems *do* get solved more easily when you have technology on your side."

Unfortunately, this problem just got more complicated. The analysis showed that the tiny glove, which was virtually indestructible, was definitely not of Earthly origin.

"Where the heck could it have come from?" asked Tim when I reported the results.

But for that, I had no answer.

"The more important question," said Rafaella, "is, What are we going to do about it?"

"Perhaps we should set a trap," I suggested.

"A trap?" asked Tim.

"Sure!" said Rafaella. "We set something up so that if anyone goes near the cage, it will sound an alarm, or take his photo, or something like that."

"But people go near the cage all day," said Tim.

"So we'll set it up so that it only works at night."

"Or," I said, "so that it only detects someone of non-Earthly origin."

"Perfect!" cried Tim.

They left it to me to design the trap. It was fairly simple: as soon as the trap detected a nonhuman presence approaching the hamster cage, it would sound an alarm, take a photograph, and spray the intruder with Feldroonian *peasquat*, a thick purple substance with a truly unfortunate smell.

"So, how are we going to install this thing?" asked Rafaella, after we had decided on what to do.

"That should be my job," said Tim. "I have to stay after school every day anyway, so I'll have the best chance."

All through the next day I watched the hamster cage for signs of unusual behavior.

The little beasts just stared back at me, blinking stupidly.

That night I called Tim to find out how he had made out with installing the trap.

"I think it was okay," he said, sounding a little nervous. "I was just finishing up when Mr. Grand walked into the room, and I had to do some fast talking to explain why I was up on the counter. But it should be all right."

I should have known then to be more nervous.

***

The Revolt of the Miniature Mutants

I was sitting in reading group the next morning, discussing a book by Natalie Babbitt called *Tuck Everlasting*, when our trap suddenly began to screech.

And who was it that set the thing off?

Jordan Lynch.

"I knew it!" cried Tim. "I knew you were an alien! Come on, take off your mask and show us your real face."

Jordan, who was now coated with horrible-smelling purple goo, was furious. "What are you talking about, you maniac?" he cried. He was about to lunge for Tim when Ms. Weintraub stepped between them. She was none too happy either.

"Just exactly what is going on here?" she asked.

The explanation was painful. It was even more painful when a simple experiment—namely, having each kid in the class go up to the cage (after I had disarmed the trap, of course) — proved that everyone in the room was capable of setting the thing off. Which meant that, unless the entire class was composed of aliens, our trap had misfired.

"I must have messed it up when Mr. Grand interrupted me," said Tim miserably.

"I'll mess you up," said Jordan in a low, menacing voice, just before he went off to the nurse's room to be cleaned up. "I was going to skip that stupid sleepover. Now I've changed my mind. It could be a lot of fun . . . for *me*!"

This obvious threat made me feel very bad. While it was possible Jordan might strike out at me, it was far more likely he would take his anger out on Tim,

The Revolt of the Miniature Mutants

who does not have the luxury of having a bodyguard.

I must say that, although the idea of needing a bodyguard horrified me when I first arrived on Earth, I have gotten used to having McNally around, and have come to rely on him a great deal.

What I have *not* gotten used to is the fact that other kids don't receive the same kind of protection. I can't understand bullies, or the people who let them do their bullying. The fact that some kids on this planet have to go to school fearing for their safety every day is something I will never understand.

Of course, Jordan's bullying was often psychological rather than physical. He would rather crush your spirit than your body. As the Grandfatherly One has said more than once, Jordan has the potential to do great evil when he matures.

In any event, his threat was something to be taken seriously. I decided to ask McNally if he would teach Tim some ways of defending himself.

My bodyguard sighed. "I'd rather try to teach him some common sense. But, yeah, I suppose it's a good idea. Have him come over to the embassy tonight and we'll get started."

CHAPTER 9

[T I M]
PERCY

I was plenty happy when Pleskit told me that McNally had invited me to the embassy for some special training in Koo Muk Dwan, the martial art form of which he is a master. I had always wanted to learn one of those cool Asian fighting techniques, but we could never afford to pay for lessons.

Since I was hoping to learn a way to send Jordan to the moon with a single blow, I was kind of disappointed when we spent the first three nights of my training with McNally telling me why it was considered a failure if I actually had to use the technique, since the goal was to avoid violence, and then having me do things

The Revolt of the Miniature Mutants

like hold my arms straight out in front of me for as long as I could to build up my endurance and my strength of mind.

(If you think that sounds easy, try it—just put your arms out in front of you and see how long you last!)

By the fourth night things started to get a little more interesting, and soon we were deep into the good stuff, all the cool holds and throws. I thought the faces and sounds you were supposed to make while you were doing all this were sort of odd, but McNally said they were part of the Koo Muk Dwan tradition, so I copied him as carefully as I could. The first time I practiced in my room at home, my mother came to the door to ask if I had a stomachache.

Despite McNally's training, I was pretty nervous by the night of the sleepover, since I wasn't sure what Jordan might be planning in terms of revenge. For this reason, I came to school more prepared than usual. I'm not talking about alien high-tech warning devices. What I had was some useful stuff to put around my sleeping bag to alert me if Jordan should come creeping up on me. ("Creep" being an appropriate word to use for any situation in which Jordan is involved.)

My security devices included: three bags of jacks, which I figured if Jordan stepped on in his bare feet would send him jumping and hollering; a pair of mouse-traps I'd snitched from my kitchen; several squeaky pet toys that would alert me if anyone stepped on them; and a roll of Bubble Wrap.

We hadn't been ignoring the hamsters all this week, of course. We just hadn't seen them doing anything suspicious. The question was, Did that mean it really had been the vitamins, and their effect was wearing off? Or did it mean the hamsters had gotten so smart, they were able to operate without tipping us off?

Pleskit and I had made a plan to slip away during the sleepover to check on them, thinking that at night was when they probably did . . . whatever they were doing.

I was choosing my spot on the gym floor—against a wall, so I would have only three sides to defend —when Pleskit and McNally showed up.

"Glad to see you," I said happily. "I was starting to worry that your Fatherly One wasn't going to let you come after all."

The Revolt of the Miniature Mutants

Pleskit smiled. "He's going to come himself later, for the midnight storytelling. And he said that as long as McNally was willing to accompany me now, it was all right with him."

I glanced at McNally. From the way he lifted his eyebrows, I got the feeling he was rolling his eyes. I couldn't see his eyes themselves, of course — they were hidden behind his dark glasses. I wondered if one reason he'd agreed to come was that Ms. Weintraub was going to be there.

"This sleepover is a great idea!" continued Pleskit enthusiastically. "It's totally . . . *cool*!" He looked at me anxiously. "Is that a proper use of the term?"

"Absolutely," I assured him.

"I even brought my air mattress," he said.

"What's the big deal?" asked Rafaella, who had come wandering over to talk with us. "Everyone has air mattresses."

"Not like Pleskit's," I replied. "He's got a mattress made out of air! That's all — just air! It's the best thing for bouncing on ever. But I didn't know they were portable," I said, turning to him.

"This was a gift from the Fatherly One. He's trying

to make up for how much he's ignored me over the last several months."

Later, when we had a minute alone, Pleskit took me aside and whispered, "Even though the Fatherly One has promised to come for the late-night storytelling, I still fear he will not actually show up."

I understood. Pleskit's Fatherly One had let him down on this kind of thing more than once. On the other hand, at least Pleskit *has* a male parental unit, which is more than I can say. "I bet he'll be here," I said.

With McNally's help we set up the air mattress and started bouncing on it. Well, of course everyone wanted to try, until finally Ms. Weintraub and some of the other teachers put a stop to it because Percy the Mad Poet had arrived and it was time for the poetry jam.

He was already standing at the microphone that was set up on the stage at the front of the room.

"You guys ready to jam?" asked Percy.

"Let's go!" we cried.

This was a call-and-response he had taught us years earlier.

"Okay," he said. "First poem."

Then he read us something called "The Rage of

The Revolt of the Miniature Mutants

the Duck." It was weird but funny. To tell you the truth, I don't think I really understood it. That's a problem I have with poetry sometimes, especially Percy's.

He did a couple more poems, then said, "All right, now it's your turn!"

Several people read poems, including Rafaella and Misty. Misty's was pretty gooey—all about love and rainbows and her aching heart. I thought Rafaella's, which was about snakes, was a lot better. For me the highlight of the whole thing was when Pleskit performed a traditional Hevi-Hevian poem, complete with farts and other bodily sounds.

He had learned enough about Earthlings by now to choose a poem that was *supposed* to be funny—which was a good thing, because people got hysterical. "It's too bad," he said sadly when I was congratulating him. "I would have preferred to do a tragic poem. I have a truly moving fart of great sorrow."

So far the evening was a big success.

The only problem was, Pleskit's Fatherly One still hadn't showed up, and I could tell Pleskit was starting to get pretty upset about it.

After the poetry jam, as things were settling down

a bit and the school was sealed for the night so that McNally was feeling fairly calm and therefore not keeping as close an eye on us as he had earlier, I went to get Pleskit. Just as we had planned, we sneaked off down the hall to check on the hamsters, to see if we could catch them being weird. We had a theory that they acted even stranger at night than they did in the daytime.

It was pretty spooky tiptoeing down those dark hallways, especially since we didn't want to get caught by anyone.

Pressing ourselves against the walls, moving in almost perfect silence, we made it safely to the room.

Then, just as we were about to go through the door, a hand came down on my shoulder.

"Just what are you two doing?" asked a voice that filled me with terror.

CHAPTER 10

[PLESKIT]
SOMETHING CHANGES

When Tim shouted and jumped, I did the same thing, and barely restrained myself from going into *kleptra.*

Before the squawk was even out of my mouth, I realized who had accosted us.

It was Jordan, as I could tell from the sound of his laugh.

We turned to face him.

He shook his head in disgust. "What a pair of wusses," he sneered. Then he narrowed his eyes and added, "Sneaky wusses at that. What are you two up to this time?"

"We're checking on the hamsters," I said. "And please let go of my friend."

Jordan was still gripping Tim's shoulder, and I could tell by the look on Tim's face that the grip was painful. The reason I could see Tim's face, even though Jordan's flashlight was not pointing directly at it, was that my *sphen-gnut-ksher* had started to spark, which cast a flickering purple glow over all three of us.

I think that may be why Jordan actually let go of Tim. He knows from personal experience that my *sphen-gnut-ksher* can emit a powerful surge of energy.

"You two are such wackoids," he said, dropping his hand. "What is it with you and these hamsters?"

I decided to take a radical step and tell Jordan the truth.

"Jordan," I said, "you know a fair amount of what has happened in the last year. If you thought about it for even a moment, you would realize that I have a powerful reason to fear hamsters. However, I do recognize that our class pets, even though they resemble my enemy Mikta-makta-mookta, are not really a menace. In order to deal with my trauma, I began feeding Doris, Ronald, and Hubert a vitamin supplement I created. It was a kind of therapy."

"Aliens must have weird psychiatrists," muttered Jordan.

Ignoring his rudeness, I continued my story. "The frightening thing is, even after I stopped giving the hamsters the supplement, they continued to change, almost as if they were mutating. I did not think the vitamins could have done that, though I am not certain. Then Tim found something strange beside their cage."

"Like what?" asked Jordan. His lip was curled in a sneer, but he was obviously interested in what I was saying.

"Like this," said Tim, taking the tiny glove out of his pocket.

Jordan snorted. "What's so strange about that? My little sister has lots of gloves that size for her doll set."

"This material is not of Earthly origin, "I said, trying to sound ominous.

Jordan looked at me for a moment, then nodded. "You know, Pleskit, things have been pretty weird in this class since you got here."

From those words, I could tell that he believed me.

I looked him straight in the eye. "I know. And I apologize. It was never my intention."

He nodded toward Tim. "So tell me—why'd you pick whackbutt here to hang out with?"

"Hey!" said Tim.

"Shut up," said Jordan.

"Tim befriended me when no one else would. Moreover, he has a sense of mankind's possibilities that I find missing in many of your people, a sense of the wonder that lies waiting in the stars. Also, he accepts people's differences quite easily." I turned the question around. "Why did you attack me that first day on the playground?"

"I didn't attack you," said Jordan. "You were the one who fried me, remember?"

"Only after you shoved him," said Tim.

"Shut up, Tompkins," said Jordan. "I'm talking to Pleskit."

"Please show Tim more respect," I said calmly.

Jordan looked at me as if . . . well, as if I were from another planet. We stared at each other for a long moment of silence. Then he said, "We'd better take a look at those hamsters."

The Revolt of the Miniature Mutants

Something had happened, but I wasn't sure what.

Jordan led the way into the classroom, since he was the one who had a flashlight.

"Oh, geez," he muttered.

"What?" cried Tim. *"What?"*

"The hamsters are gone."

"I don't like the look of this," said Tim nervously.

"If you two have been messing with me, you're not going to like the look of your face when I'm done with you, Tompkins," said Jordan, who clearly felt we had been playing him for a fool.

He took a step toward Tim. But before he could touch him, a tiny voice — harsh but feminine — said sharply, "Put your hands up and don't move!"

CHAPTER 11

[TIM]
MUTANT HAMSTERS

We spun around.

Standing on a desk behind us were three furry creatures, each about four or five inches high. They looked
a lot like our class hamsters, except for three things:

1. They had longer arms and legs, and were clearly
comfortable standing up.

2. They were wearing shiny orange uniforms, complete with belts and boots.

3. Clutched in their tiny, long-fingered paws were
bright, futuristic-looking ray guns.

I stared at them in astonishment. "Doris?" I asked
warily. "Ronald? Hubert?"

The Revolt of the Miniature Mutants

"Nailed it on your first try, Buster," snarled Doris, who seemed to be the leader. "So whaddaya want, a medal? Now get your hands up or you'll see what these ray guns can do. Come on, move those paws!"

Pleskit and I put our hands up.

"You too, pretty boy," snapped Doris, aiming her ray gun directly at Jordan. "You didn't think I'd forget the way you stuffed me into Pleskit's lunchbox, did you?"

"I take back what I said before," muttered Jordan, slowly raising his hands. "You two aren't wackoids. You're *maniacs*! What did you—"

"Quiet!" ordered Doris. "Hubert, keep an eye on them while I talk with Ronald."

"Okee-bedokee, Doree," said Hubert, who clearly had not picked up the basics of human speech as well as Doris had.

"Don't call me 'Doree'!" snapped Doris. "Call me 'Chief'!"

"Youbah gottit . . . Chief!" said Hubert, smiling foolishly.

Doris and Ronald trotted back to the far side of the desk and put their heads together. A few minutes later they came back. Doris was smiling. "Well, we've got the perfect solution."

"Solution for what?" asked Jordan nervously.

"For what to do with you three. The big boss thought something like this might happen. Now we have our substitutes."

"Substitutes?" I asked nervously.

"Quiet, human!" said Doris again. Then she blasted us with a purple beam from her ray gun.

We froze in place, unable to move.

Now it was Ronald's turn to use his ray gun. The ray from his gun was crimson, and when he pointed it at us, we began to shrink. My innards felt as if they were folding in on themselves. The walls seemed to shoot up around us. For a moment my eyes were blurred by a red haze. When I could see again, it was as if I had been dropped onto a movie set constructed for giants.

Except the classroom hadn't changed. We had.

We were now just the same size as the hamsters.

"Get the suits," said Doris.

Ronald and Hubert ran off. They didn't scamper, as you might expect of a hamster; they *ran* off, on their hind legs.

The Revolt of the Miniature Mutants

I wondered what kind of suits they were going for.

A few minutes later I got my answer, and it was pretty horrifying. The suits that Ronald and Hubert had been sent for were . . . *hamster* suits!

"All right, get out of your clothes and put these on," said Doris.

"You've got to be kidding," said Jordan.

Her ray gun drilled a smoking hole into the floor next to Jordan's foot. "This thing has seventy-two different settings," she growled, "including wide-angle stun. Now strip and get into these suits!"

I looked around uneasily. I didn't really want to undress in front of Jordan and Pleskit — not to mention Doris (who, despite being a hamster, was still a female, after all).

"Next ray doesn't hit the floor," said Doris.

Jordan turned his back to us and started to strip. I did the same thing. I assume Pleskit did too, though I don't know, since I wasn't watching. When I was half-undressed, I turned back to grab the hamster suit that I was supposed to wear.

"That one's me!" said Hubert proudly. "Webuh wore them after we begunna change, so no people

The Revolt of the Miniature Mutants

things woubba notice us. The boss said —"

"Shut up, blabbermouth!" ordered Doris.

I glanced over my shoulder at Hubert. He had put his paws over his face and was looking embarrassed.

"Keep moving," said Doris ominously.

I finished undressing. I slipped one leg into the hamster suit, then the other. To my astonishment, as soon as I had also put in both arms, the suit finished the job, sliding over me as if it were swallowing me.

"Hey!" I cried. "What the —"

My words were cut off by the hamster headpiece that slid over my face. Before I could move, the suit *sealed itself up.* Then I heard a tiny hissing sound. Later I realized it was from little air sacs that had started inflating. They filled out the suit, locking me in more tightly and at the same time changing the suit's outer contours to make it look exactly like Hubert. The feeling was weird. Hamster arms and legs are much shorter than a human's, so it was really only my hands and feet that were in the arms and legs of the suit. From the wrists and ankles back, I was held in place by the inflated air sacs.

What made all of this truly terrifying was that I

couldn't find any way to open the suit, any way to get out of it.

I looked around. Pleskit was wearing the Ronald suit—which meant that Jordan got to be Doris. I thought this seemed like a good match of personalities.

"I'm going to get you two for this," Jordan said bitterly.

To my surprise, the words didn't come out of his mouth—or, to be more precise, the mouth of his suit. I heard them through a tiny speaker system built right into my own suit.

Well, at least we would be able to communicate with one another.

"I wonder how long they're planning on keeping us in these things?" I said nervously.

I thought I was just talking to Jordan and Pleskit. To my horror, Doris answered me. I wondered at first how she had heard me. Then I figured out that she was probably wearing an earpiece set to pick up what we said.

Her answer sent a cold chill down my spine. "How long?" she asked smoothly, "I don't know for sure. Probably forever."

The Revolt of the Miniature Mutants

It took a second for her words to sink in. Then I felt a blinding panic.

Forever?

My fear subsided when I realized that that was impossible. We had used a shrinking ray before, and I knew that the compression technique took so much power that eventually the rays would wear off and we would return to our normal size. She was just toying with us.

As if she were reading my mind, Doris said, "And don't think you're going to grow back in just a few hours. We know all about the shrinking ray Pleskit and Tim used a while back. That was a mere desk toy. This one is far more powerful. It even manages the mass-weight problem quite nicely. Right now you weigh no more than we do — which means no one will be able to tell the difference when they pick you up."

She smiled. I had never realized a hamster's face could look so frightening.

"The point of all this, of course, is that you three are going to replace us in the classroom. Lovely, isn't it? With you here, no one will realize that we've become . . . something else. And no one will ever begin to suspect what has become of the three missing boys! Who would think to look for them in . . . a hamster cage?"

"Don't worry, guys," said Ronald cheerfully. "It's not a bad life, being a hamster! All the pellets you can eat, a free exercise wheel, and fresh shavings whenever the kids happen to remember."

"Shut up!" said Doris, smacking him in the back of the head. "You three — move! Into the cage!"

"Yeah," said Ronald sullenly, rubbing the spot where Doris had hit him. "Into the cage."

We would have been too short to get into the cage, except that while Doris had been talking to us, Hubert had been shoving around some books to make a little stairway that led right up the side.

"*Move!*" snarled Doris, sizzling another energy blast next to my feet. "Hubert, gather up their clothes. We don't want to leave them around as clues!"

"Etcha youbetcha, Dor . . . uh, *Chief*," said Hubert.

I watched him scoop up my tiny clothes. Then I sighed and began to climb the book stairway—the stairway that seemed to lead to a life with me permanently disguised as a hamster.

CHAPTER 12

[PLESKIT]
CUDDLED

My hamster suit was hot and cramped, and difficult to move in. I stumbled more than once as I tried to climb the book staircase.

"Hurry up!" snapped Doris, impatient at my clumsy delays. I scrambled until I was standing next to Tim at the edge of the cage.

"All right, now jump in," ordered Doris.

Tim didn't move.

"You heard me!" she shrieked, firing a hot needle of light to convince him. "Jump!"

Tim jumped.

Jordan and I followed, even though the jump was

about four times our current height, which made it terrifying to do. To my surprise, the landing was fairly gentle. At first I thought it was because the wood shavings provided a cushion. Then I realized the truth, and felt like an idiot. I knew enough science to have figured out *before* we jumped that at our current weight the impact would not be that bad.

"I can't believe what you two have gotten me into," said Jordan furiously. "If we ever get out of—"

He was interrupted by some activity at the top of the cage. We looked up. Ronald and Hubert had climbed the stack of books. Now each of them was swinging a line with a purple blob on the end of it. Ronald counted to three and they threw the lines. The blobs hit the top of the cage and stuck fast, as if they were coated with glue. Immediately the two miniature mutants began walking back down the book stairway, pulling the cage top into place as they went.

I watched in dread as the dark plastic slid over us. Then, just an instant before the top was completely in place, Doris said urgently, "There's someone coming!"

It was amazing how fast those hamsters could move. Ronald and Hubert each touched a button on their

The Revolt of the Miniature Mutants

belts, which somehow disconnected their purple blobs from the cage top. Then they threw the lines again. The purple blobs stuck on the side of Chris Mellblom's desk.

"Bombs away!" cried Ronald as he and Hubert leaped off the counter and swung down to the floor. A second later the purple blobs disappeared from the side of the desk—pulled in by whatever winding mechanism they had on their lines.

"Just like Batman," murmured Tim in awe.

"Spoken like a true moron," said Jordan.

I looked around for Doris, but she had disappeared as well.

Suddenly the room lights came on, dazzling us with their brightness. I turned toward the door and felt a surge of hope.

It was Rafaella and Larrabe!

"Huh," said Rafaella, looking around. "I was sure Tim and Pleskit would be in here. I can't figure out where else they might have gone." She paused, then added angrily, "I still can't believe they took off without me!"

"We're here!" I cried. "Right over here, Rafaella!"

But no words came out, of course. The suits made it impossible for us to speak. I reared up on my hind legs, waving my tiny arms. Tim and Jordan joined me.

"Those two are always taking off and hiding somewhere," said Larrabe, a trifle bitterly. "Come on, Raf— let's go back to the gym."

"No, no! We're here!" cried all three of us, so desperate that we ignored the fact that there was no way they could hear us. "Look over here!"

They were turning to go when Rafaella noticed us waving.

"Look at the hamsters," she said. "At least they're glad to see us, Larrabe. Aren't they cute?"

Larrabe and Rafaella are probably the only two people in our class who would think three hamsters standing on their hind legs and waving their paws were doing so because the hamsters were glad to see them.

They came over to the cage.

"Uh-oh," said Larrabe when he saw that the top was not properly in place. "Looks like they were planning a breakout!"

"We'd better move these books," said Rafaella. "If they ever did get the top off, they could climb down and get away. I wonder what idiot left the books here like this."

The Revolt of the Miniature Mutants

"Noooo!" cried Jordan as Larrabe shifted the books away from the cage. "Put those back, you moron!"

The words rang in my ears. Rafaella and Larrabe, of course, couldn't hear a thing.

"These guys are looking pretty normal," said Larrabe, crouching down to stare into the cage. "Whatever Pleskit did to them must have worn off."

"Yeah," agreed Rafaella. "They just look like regular hamsters now." She pried off the top of the cage that Larrabe had just pushed down and reached in to pick up Tim. "Aren't you a cutie," she said, holding him up so that his nose was touching hers.

Larrabe picked up Jordan and did the same thing. "Whose ickle hamster is oo?" he said in a gooey voice.

"Put me down!" shrieked Jordan —words that Tim and I could hear, but Rafaella and Larrabe could not.

"Boy, Doris is squirmy tonight," said Larrabe. "What's wrong with you, baby?"

He turned Jordan over and looked at his stomach.

"What are you doing?" asked Rafaella.

"I was just trying to see if she's pregnant," said Larrabe.

"I'm not pregnant!" cried Jordan furiously.

"Come on," said Rafaella, dropping Tim back into the cage. "We'd better get going."

Larrabe dropped Jordan in beside me, then put the top firmly back on the cage.

"Make sure that's on tight," said Rafaella.

Larrabe pressed the top all around the edges to seal it securely.

Then the two of them left the room.

We were alone in our hamster suits again.

CHAPTER 13

[JORDAN]
HAMSTER SCHEMES

Okay, this is me, Jordan. I can't believe I'm writing this, but since I was one of the kids who got trapped in those stupid hamster suits, and since Ms. Weintraub said she would give me extra credit and wipe out the last three Fs I got in English if I did, I decided to go for it.

(The Fs weren't because I didn't know the stuff, in case you were wondering. They were for not handing in work.)

Anyway, the first thing I want to say is that I couldn't believe what those two wackbutts had gotten me into. I would have clobbered both of them, except those stupid hamster suits were not made for clobbering.

"If we ever get out of this, you guys are going to pay big-time," I said. "My father will sue you for all you're worth — which isn't much in your case, Tompkins."

"Why are you so hostile?" asked Pleskit — which was just like him. You can tell he's an alien. I mean, there we were, four inches high and in danger of spending the rest of our lives as imitation hamsters, and he wanted to psychoanalyze me.

"I'm trapped in a hamster suit and it's your fault!" I cried. "What do you think I'm going to do — kiss you?"

"But you have been hostile since the day I arrived," said Pleskit. "I'd like to know why."

I started to answer him, then realized I didn't really *have* a good answer, which was kind of embarrassing. "This is a stupid time to ask a question like that," I said.

Fortunately for me, Tim piped up with his own stupidness.

"Jordan has always believed in hassling anyone who's different," he said.

It was a relief to have him say something so typically dippy. "You don't think *I'm* different?" I asked.

"I suppose you are," he said. "It must be really

The Revolt of the Miniature Mutants

heartbreaking to be tall, good-looking, and rich. I feel your pain."

I almost answered him for real. Almost. But I don't tell that kind of stuff. And I'm not about to tell you, whoever you are reading this, either. That's my own stuff, and it's private. So I just said, "Shut up, Tim. If it weren't for you and Pleskit, we wouldn't be trapped here like this anyway."

"If you hadn't followed us just to hassle us, you wouldn't be here now," said Tim. "So it serves you right."

I was looking for a searing comeback when the real hamsters, or the miniature mutants, or whatever they were, stepped out of hiding.

"Willbuh mighty leader be backcoming soon, do you think?" asked Hubert, who was the dippiest of the three as far as I was concerned.

"Who do you think the leader is?" asked Tim quietly. "Could it be Mikta-makta-mookta?"

"Not possible," said Pleskit. "The embassy receives constant reports on her, and she is still in custody. Even if she had escaped in the last couple of days, she would not have had time to get here and organize this plot. It must be someone else."

"Shhh!" I said. "Let's listen."

It turned out their plan had two parts. First, their "mighty leader" wanted to get revenge on Pleskit—which they had pretty much accomplished, if you consider shrinking someone and locking him in a hamster suit revenge, which I definitely do.

Second, they were going to do something to sabotage his old man's mission.

"Who cares what they do to the mission," I said. "I just want to get out of this stupid hamster suit."

"Listen, Jordan," said Tim. "There are a few things you ought to know."

"Like what?" I sneered.

Then he told me some stuff that astonished me, about how Pleskit's Fatherly One was a benevolent Trader and wanted to work to help Earth develop itself, but if he lost his claim on the planet, the next Traders to take over might be horrible colonizers who would just suck the planet dry—and they would be allowed to do so, because from the point of view of the galactic leaders, we were just a barbaric, uncivilized planet headed for self-destruction anyway.

The Revolt of the Miniature Mutants

"Good grief!" I cried. "That's horrible!"

Before Tim could reply, we heard a flurry of excitement from the hamsters.

"The boss!" cried Ronald. "It's the boss. The boss is here!"

CHAPTER 14

[TIM]
"THE BOSS"

I felt a shiver of recognition when the hamsters' "boss" came sauntering up to our cage. He was a hamster too — or, at least, a hamsteroid-type being. And I had seen him once before, back when Linnsy was still here. He had appeared to the two of us as a holographic figure — human-size, not hamster height, as he was now — and had told us to beware of Ellico *vec* Bur. Obviously, it had been a false warning, since Ellico *vec* Bur had turned out to be pretty good beings, while this guy was clearly a deadly enemy.

"Greetings, gentlemen," he said now, running his

paws over his whiskers. "How nice to find you in such a cozy situation."

"Who is this jerk?" asked Jordan.

I could hear Jordan, of course, because of the inter-suit communication system. But I didn't expect the hamsteroid "boss" to be able to. However, he must have been wearing a receiver also, since he answered the question.

"You can call me Wiktor. My full name is Wiktor-waktor-wooktor." He smiled, a pretty horrifying sight when made by a malevolent hamsteroid. "I believe Tim and Pleskit have already met my littersister, Mikta-makta-mookta."

Suddenly everything made horrible sense—and Pleskit's seemingly absurd fear of hamsters was completely justified.

"In fact," continued Wiktor, his voice suddenly angry, "I believe those two interfering little nuisances have made my littersister's life quite miserable over the last year. Now it's time for me to return the favor."

He turned to the hamsterly trio. "I'm delighted to see that you have Pleskit and his idiot friend in custody. But who's in the third suit?"

"His name is Jordan," said Doris. "He is an evil presence in the classroom. It is unlikely he will be missed."

"Hey!" said Jordan. "What did I ever do to —"

He stopped, clearly remembering the lunchbox incident.

Doris gave him a blood-chilling smile. "We watch," she replied. "We listen. We remember. And we know you for what you are."

Jordan whimpered.

Clever hamsters, I thought, feeling a surge of affection for them despite the fact that they had captured us.

"Well done," said Wiktor. "Now it's time for another treatment. Are you ready, my little ones?"

I wasn't sure, at first, whether he was referring to the hamsters or to us, until Ronald whined, "Do we have to?"

"Yes, you have to," said Wiktor sharply, "unless you want to revert to the seed-grubbing idiots you were when I first met you." He turned to the cage where we stood watching and added, "As you have probably guessed by now, I have been working with this oppressed species, which is obviously downtrodden by the human population of this planet."

The Revolt of the Miniature Mutants

He held up a ray gun, bigger and fancier than the ones the hamsters had been using. "This is the Human Attribute Maximization, Strength Treatment, and Energy Raising Ray—or, as I call it for short, the HAMSTER Ray!" He chuckled. "Purely an Earth joke, of course. But as we say on my planet, when in Fleegle, do as the Fleegelians do."

"Then it wasn't my vitamin treatment that mutated them?" cried Pleskit, sounding relieved.

"Well, your vitamins helped," said Wiktor. "But that was just a lucky coincidence. They wouldn't have come along nearly as fast without them." He gestured toward the hamsters. "However, I need to give them repeated treatments in order for them to retain the advances they have made. Fortunately, the effect is cumulative—these poor primitives get a little brighter and a little stronger each time I give them a treatment. Another few doses and the changes will be permanent." He turned back to the hamsters. "All right, my dears—line up!"

With a little pushing and shoving from Doris, the hamsters got in line.

Wiktor pulled the trigger on his ray gun.

Instantly the hamsters were bathed in a bright lavender ray.

"Thabbit tiggles!" cried Hubert, just before he fell over backward. Then he began to shriek, a horrible, high-pitched whistling sound that hurt my ears.

Soon all three of the hamsteroids were lying on the counter, twitching helplessly. They looked as if they were being electrocuted. But Wiktor just kept pointing the ray at them, laughing as he did.

Despite what they had done to us, I felt that Doris, Ronald, and Hubert were also victims of Wiktor—that they had only captured and shrunk us because they were under his control. My stomach tightened as I watched them twitch and jerk as if they were dying.

"Stop it!" I cried. "Stop, Wiktor! You're killing them!"

"No pain, no gain!" said Wiktor, laughing madly. He turned a dial on the ray gun. The light grew more intense, the twitching and writhing of the hamsters worse than ever.

Then, suddenly, he turned off the ray.

The hamsters lay there for a long moment, still twitching occasionally. Suddenly Doris sat up, then sprang to her feet. I could tell just by looking at her that she was bigger and stronger than ever.

"That always makes me itch like crazy, " she said, scratching behind one ear. "But when it's done, I feel fantastic!"

"Mebuh tuba!" said Hubert, pushing himself to his feet and flexing his muscles. He stopped, looking puzzled. "But mebums don't feel noble smarter."

"You can't have everything," said Wiktor with a sigh.

"I'm hungry," said Ronald.

"You always gots the hongries," said Hubert. "Youbums should save more food for when youbums needles it."

"Shut up, you two," said Doris. "We've got work to do." She turned to Wiktor. "What's next, Boss?"

Wiktor laughed. "Next? Next we put an end to Meenom Ventrah's 'friendly' mission."

"How we gonna do it, Boss?" asked Ronald.

Wiktor smiled. "Our little friend Pleskit has talked his Fatherly One into attending tonight's gathering. So everyone will be expecting him. Unfortunately — unfortunately for Pleskit — Meenom also had to attend a little meeting in Japan this evening. I have managed to arrange for a delay in his return. I'm going to — "

Before he could finish explaining his plan, we heard a noise outside the classroom.

"Intruder alert!" cried Ronald.

The hamsters and Wiktor dived for cover. Jordan, Pleskit, and I pressed our faces to the side of the cage so we could see who was coming. I was filled with hope for our rescue, yet at the same time was terrified it might be Larrabe and Rafaella again and that Wiktor would do something terrible to them.

So I was thrilled to see McNally at the door. Maybe we were going to get out of this after all!

"Pleskit?" he called, standing at the doorway. He sounded annoyed. "Pleskit, where the heck are you?"

We beat the walls of our cage and waved our little paws, trying to attract his attention. But before McNally could spot us, the hamsters attacked!

CHAPTER 15

[P L E S K I T]
DISGUISE

Though my *smorgle* lifted with hope when McNally came through the door, that hope turned to horror when I heard Doris cry, "Hamsters away!"

They had flung their lines so that the purple blobs stuck to the light fixtures. Now they launched themselves in a crosswise swing, like a trio of circus acrobats.

"What the —" cried McNally as Ronald and Hubert swung past him. Doris let go of her line and landed on his shoulder. Pulling out her ray gun, she gave him a quick blast.

His knees buckled and he fell to the floor.

I cried out in horror, and not just because McNally

was our last hope. He was also my true and good friend, and I did not want to see him hurt.

"Well done, my pretties!" cried Wiktor as he scampered over to McNally to be sure he was really out.

It made me sick to see Wiktor climbing over McNally's face.

After a moment he scurried back to the hamsterly trio. "All right," he said, "time for me to return to normal." He made an adjustment to his ray gun, then handed it to Doris. "Hit me, baby!" he cried.

"You got it, Big Daddy!" replied Doris.

This struck me as being vaguely sickening.

Doris stepped back a few feet, then pulled the trigger.

A shimmering orange ray shot out from the gun and surrounded Wiktor. Thirty seconds later he was at his full height again — about five and a half feet tall.

When Wiktor had been hamster-size, he could not have bound and gagged McNally, of course. Now it was no problem for him. It was also, in a way, an enormous relief for me. That Wiktor was bothering to do so meant that Doris had only stunned McNally, and Wiktor expected him to recover eventually.

The Revolt of the Miniature Mutants

Once Wiktor had McNally completely trussed up, he dragged him behind Ms. Weintraub's desk. He pulled out her chair, stuffed McNally into the space beneath the desk that was meant for her legs, and then pushed the chair as far back into place as it would go.

"That will keep *him* out of the way for the time being," Wiktor said, sounding satisfied. He turned back to the hamsterly trio. "All right, you three have your orders. Get moving. I have to get ready for my part."

In the back corner of the room was a pipe, about an inch and a half in diameter, that ran from the floor up through the ceiling. I assumed it was part of the heating system. Whatever it was, Doris, Ronald, and Hubert scuttled up it and squeezed their way through the hole where the pipe entered the ceiling.

As they were leaving, Wiktor opened his pack and took out several items.

"My disguise for the evening," he said, glancing over at us.

I couldn't help but think of the time when Mikta-makta-mookta had dressed up as a school inspector in an attempt to kidnap Tim and me to pay us back for foiling her first plan to destroy the Fatherly

One's mission. I wondered who Wiktor was going to pretend to be.

"How did you get into the school to begin with?" asked Tim as our captor was putting on his outfit. "Security is even tighter than usual tonight."

Wiktor, who was standing with his back to us, laughed. "Human adults tend to ignore the small stuff. It would never occur to them to look for someone four inches tall. So I just landed on the roof of the building and squirmed through a small opening I made weeks ago." He paused to make a final adjustment to his costume, then said, "And now it's time for me to put an end to your Fatherly One's mission, Pleskit."

He turned around.

We gasped in horror, even Jordan.

Wiktor had disguised himself as the Fatherly One!

He strolled over to the cage and pressed his fake face to the clear wall. The disguise was horrifyingly accurate. I think it would have fooled even me if I had not known who it was.

"I assume you recognize me, Pleskit," Wiktor sneered. "Actually, I'm confident the whole school will know who I am. So they'll be able to confirm just who it

was that did . . . well, what I am about to do. This may be the last time I see you boys. I wish you long and healthy lives in your cozy little hamster suits!"

He laughed hysterically.

Then he turned and left the room.

He switched off the lights as he went, leaving us alone in the dark.

CHAPTER 16

[T I M]
HUBERT

After Wiktor left, none of us said a thing for several minutes. We just sat in the dark, imprisoned in our little hamster suits, nursing our terror.

I was the one who finally broke the silence.

"I don't get it," I said, trying not to whine. "Why do these things always happen to us?"

"Because you're so weird!" snapped Jordan. His voice was ragged with fear and desperation.

"Well, since you're along this time, must be you're weird too," I replied quickly.

"Why don't you just shut up, Tompkins," said Jordan. I could tell from his voice that he was trying not to cry.

"Don't worry," said Pleskit, patting him on the shoulder. "We'll get out of this somehow."

"Leave me alone, you purple freak!" Jordan snapped, wrenching away from Pleskit's hand.

Pleskit came to stand beside me.

The two of us have been in tough spots before. But I don't think either of us has ever felt as helpless as we did trapped in those stupid hamster suits.

"What are we going to do?" moaned Jordan a few minutes later. He got up and began pacing around the cage. Finally he flung himself against one of the clear walls and began beating on it with his tiny paws.

"Let us out of here!" he screamed. "Let us out!"

I think he has watched too many old prison movies.

"Well, at least he's including *us* in that request," whispered Pleskit.

Unfortunately, the inter-suit communication system allowed Jordan to hear this comment. "Shut up!" he snarled.

Then he went into a corner of the cage, curled up into a ball, and began to sob.

Neither Pleskit nor I said a thing, partly because whatever we said, Jordan would hear. (I was glad we could communicate, but this total sharing was getting to be a pain.)

The sound of his weeping only reinforced the terror of the situation.

"I am deeply concerned about the Fatherly One," said Pleskit, reminding me that we weren't the only ones in a bad situation. "What do you suppose Wiktor is intending to do?"

"Whatever it is, it's going to be bad," I said.

Then there was nothing more to say, so we just sat in gloomy silence. I was actually nodding off to sleep — it had been an exhausting night — when I heard someone knocking on the wall of the cage.

It was Hubert!

"Shhbus!" he said. "Hubie comes to get goodle boyses out of cage."

"Why?" I asked.

"Mr. Timbletoes was always kind to hamsters," he said. "Hubert wabbans returna the favor. Besides, I am not liking Wiktor tuba much, even if he does make hamsters smarter and stronger. Mostly stronger for Hubert. Wiktor yells an orkle lot."

"Does Doris know what you're doing?" I asked.

Hubert shuddered and glanced nervously over his shoulder. "Doris poopy face would dooba something terribibble to Hubert if she knew. Now come on, we gotta stop Wiktor's badness."

Hubert took out his ray gun and made an adjustment. "Stabban back!" he ordered.

He didn't have to tell us twice, no matter how oddly he said it. We pressed ourselves to the side wall.

Hubert pulled the trigger. The ray gun emitted a needle-thin yellow ray. It took only seconds for Hubert to outline a large oval in the cage wall.

As soon as he turned off the ray, I rushed forward and pushed on the oval.

It popped out with no trouble, leaving a perfect escape route. I scrambled through the opening. Pleskit was right behind me, Jordan close on his heels.

It still wasn't that easy to move in our hamster suits, so we didn't exactly "scamper." Even so, I was starting to get used to the thing.

"I just hope no one steps on us," said Jordan.

"You can go back into the cage if you want," said Pleskit.

The Revolt of the Miniature Mutants

He was speaking quite earnestly, but Jordan took it the wrong way.

"Shut up!" he snapped.

On the other hand, he didn't call us any insulting names, so it seemed like progress.

"What now?" I said to Hubert.

"We gots to stop Wiktor."

"That would be easier if we weren't still hamster-size and stuck in these suits," I said.

"Don't be bonehead," said Hubert. "We gots to try anyway. Follow me!"

"Wait!" cried Pleskit. "We need to check on McNally first."

"Already buddit it," said Hubert. "McNally man sound buhsleep. Hubert bit up his ropes. If he wubbakes up, he can get free. Now come on, follow Hubert!"

Then he hurried off toward the pipe he and the others had climbed earlier.

We followed.

"I don't like heights," said Jordan when we got to the pipe.

"You can stay here," I offered.

"Shut up, Tim," said Jordan.

"Youbuh oughtta learn new words, Jordan," said Hubert. "Now, follow me."

He started up the pipe. I went next, grabbing the pipe with my tiny arms and legs. The suit turned out to have fairly good gripping powers. I wondered, for a second, why Wiktor would have given us suits that were so useful for moving around in, then remembered that the suits had first been designed to let Hubert, Doris, and Ronald disguise themselves when their mutations got more obvious.

Clinging to the pipe, I inched my way toward the ceiling. It was only about ten feet above the floor, but I think we must be used to measuring things in comparison to our own bodies, because when you're four inches high, ten feet suddenly looks like a very long way down.

A *very* long way.

"Keep following," said Hubert when we reached the top of the pipe. I could see a narrow hole where the pipe disappeared into the ceiling tile. Hubert squeezed into it, though I could see he had a bit of trouble getting his butt through. I followed him. I

The Revolt of the Miniature Mutants

had the same trouble with the butt of my suit, since it was designed to look just like Hubert — or, to be more precise, like he had looked before Wiktor had started treating him with the HAMSTER Ray.

I wriggled my way into the ceiling, and complete darkness.

CHAPTER 17

[PLESKIT]
INTO THE CEILING

It was tight squeezing through that hole in the ceiling, and I was afraid my butt—or, to be more specific, the butt of my hamster suit—wouldn't fit through. (Remember, I was dressed as Ronald Roundbutt, so I had the biggest hind end of the three of us.)

It took a lot of squirming, but I finally made it, just in time to hear Jordan complaining about how dark it was.

Hubert scurried over. "Izzit costume bad for seeing, or duzzit you just gots bad eyes?" he asked, sounding very concerned.

"We are not made for seeing in the dark," I said.

The Revolt of the Miniature Mutants

"Seeds and pellets!" exclaimed Hubert, sounding astonished at such an idea. "That be sillicious! Okee bedokee, waiting some minoomits while I fixxit light ray."

I heard him fiddling with his ray gun. Suddenly a bright yellow beam lit the space we had climbed into.

"Fixxit lightup!" he said proudly.

"Thanks, Hubert," I replied. "You're a pal."

"We gottsa go," he said. "Followim my butt."

We followed. The mutant hamster led us across the ceiling tiles and into a small shaft that was terrifyingly narrow. We had to squeeze to get into it, and the fear that we would never get back out was tremendous. I wondered if Hubert was leading us into a trap, but didn't want to say it out loud for fear of offending him. (Remember, he could hear anything we said because of the inter-suit comm system.)

"Wub-orry not," said Hubert, as if he were reading my mind. "Hamsters knows the way!"

It's hard to say how far we traveled, since being only four inches long completely messed up my sense of distance. I only know that Hubert led us for what seemed like miles through the walls of the building in our search for Wiktor.

We traveled by hamster routes, of course, wriggling through holes, crawling along pipes, squeezing into spaces that seemed impossibly small. Though I was eager for us to regain our true size, I began to hope that Doris was right about the shrinking ray not wearing off.

I hoped it even more when Hubert brought us to a lead pipe.

"Doris cubbut the end offa this!" he said, just before he squirmed into it.

We followed him.

The inside of that pipe was the darkest, tightest place I have ever been. And all I could think about was what might happen if the shrinking ray did wear off and I suddenly started returning to my real size while I was trapped inside it. (Even thinking about it now makes me shudder.)

Shortly after we left the pipe — one of the biggest reliefs of my life — we came to a thick mass of fluffy pink stuff, about the color of the Earthling chewable called bubble gum.

"What's this?" I asked, alarmed at the sight of it.

"It looks familiar," said Tim. "But I can't quite figure it out."

The Revolt of the Miniature Mutants

"It's insulation," said Jordan. "It's made out of fiberglass."

"Bad, bad, nasty stuff," said Hubert. "Gives hamsterses little sticky things in their skin if they tries to gebbit through it. Bad for nests. Bad for eating. Not got much sense to it. Got to go over or under. Little people follow Hubert!"

With that he plunged into a tiny dark tunnel that led under the pink stuff.

The tunnel made crinkling sounds as we traveled.

"What is that noise?" I asked in alarm.

"Insulation is lined with paper," said Jordan. "That's what we're crawling under, the paper lining."

Finally we came out of the tunnel. By the light of Hubert's ray gun we could see that we had come to the edge of whatever room we had been crawling over. There was an open area between the wall of that room and the next one. It was only a few inches away, of course, but it seemed like several feet to us. And between the walls was an opening. For us, it was like standing at the edge of a cliff with a great emptiness yawning beneath us.

"How do you know about all these paths?" asked

Jordan, gazing over the edge and shuddering.

"Hamsters been scouting building for last weekle or so," explained Hubert. "Hamsters leave cage bat night and make sure tuba back inside before children things arrives inna morning." He paused, then added proudly, "Hubert gotses little bunches of food allover school building. Makes Hubert feel safe and happy."

"Well, you can stop feeling that way right now," said a harsh voice.

"Doris!" cried Hubert in terror. "Where is she? Where is she?"

Before any of us could answer, could even begin to figure out the answer, Doris and Ronald jumped us.

CHAPTER 18

[JORDAN]
HAMSTER WRASSLIN'

As I stood at the edge of that horrible drop listening to Hubert babble, I heard a bloodcurdling cry.

Then I felt a thump on my back.

It was Ronald!

I never thought I'd be involved in a hand-to-hand, life-and-death struggle with a hamster, but there it was. I fought back with all my might.

The little beast was stronger than I would have expected, but the idea of being beaten by a hamster gave me added strength of my own, since I didn't think I could have survived the embarrassment if I lost the fight.

Or maybe it was just the adrenaline rush of wrestling

at the edge of that gaping darkness. Because the first thing that happened when Ronald hit me was that I staggered forward. We stood for a moment, tottering at the edge of the wall. Finally I arched my back and threw us away from it. We landed with Ronald underneath me. I could hear from his "Ooof!" that the fall had knocked the breath out of him. Even so, he had his arms locked around my neck. I squirmed out of his grip, then flung myself back on top of him.

He recovered his breath all too quickly. We began a desperate wrestling match.

"Jordan, watch out!" cried Tim.

I glanced to my side. We were almost at the edge of the wall again. I struggled harder than ever, trying to push us away from it. Ronald seemed to have no fear— though whether that was because he knew a hamster could survive such a fall or he was just too stupid to be afraid, I wasn't sure.

"Oh, bad, bad, bad," moaned Hubert, who was watching all this without moving, just wringing his paws and moaning.

"Shut up and help!" I ordered.

Not that I really wanted to be helped by a mutant

hamster. But when you're caught in hand-to-hand combat at the edge of a drop into bottomless darkness, you find you're willing to accept help wherever you can find it.

As it worked out, I experienced something even worse than being helped by a hamster.

I was helped by Tim.

Ronald had me right at the edge of the wall and was forcing me forward when from behind us I heard, "Oooeeyee fah wooeeoo!"

Then Tim kicked Ronald in the butt, which was about as high as his stumpy hamster costume legs would let him reach. Tim fell over from making the kick. I didn't make fun of him the way I usually would have, since that kick was all I needed to get the best of Ronald.

While Ronald and I were still struggling, Tim got back to his feet. I realized that he and Pleskit were both fighting with Doris. I'll be glad to admit that she was more dangerous than Ronald — definitely a two-man job. When I finally got Ronald firmly pinned, I shouted for Hubert. "Get over here and sit on him!" I ordered. "Now!"

As soon as Hubert was in place, I scooped up

The Revolt of the Miniature Mutants

Ronald's ray gun. "All right, Doris," I said fiercely. "Game's over."

She glanced up, then raised her paws.

"Get her ray gun, Pleskit," I said.

He took it from her, then said, "All right, where's Wiktor now? Has he gone into the gym yet?"

"What makes you think I'll tell you?" she sneered.

"You heard Pleskit," I said. "Where's Wiktor?"

"I don't talk for pretty boys, either," she snapped.

And she didn't, not even when I threatened to push her over the edge, which seemed to horrify those sissies Tim and Pleskit. You'd think they had forgotten we were in a struggle not just for our lives but for the safety of the planet.

I had to admire Doris. She was the toughest hamster I'd ever met.

Fortunately, Ronald was easier to convince. I think maybe he had a crush on Doris, because when I was threatening her, he was the one who broke down.

"Wiktor is in the gymnasium!" he said. "Now let her go, will you?"

"Shut up, you sniveling excuse for a hamster!" said Doris.

She reminded me a lot of my mother.

"What's Wiktor going to do?" asked Pleskit.

"Don't tell them!" ordered Doris.

"He's going to kidnap Ms. Weintraub," sobbed Ronald.

"Weakling!" sneered Doris, smacking him on the back of the head.

"Good grief!" cried Pleskit. "That's fiendish!"

It took me a second to figure it out; then I realized he was right. If Wiktor/Meenom had done something horrible to one of the kids, or all of them, for that matter, it would have been so out of character that most people would have found it unbelievable, and suspected a plot of some kind right from the beginning. But with all the publicity that the *Scoop* had started about Meenom being a woman-crazed alien, all too many people would be willing to believe he truly had stolen our teacher—who is, after all, hot.

"We've got to stop him!" cried Pleskit.

"But how do we get to the gym from here?" asked Tim.

To our surprise, Ronald said, "I'll take you."

"What are you doing, you traitor?" shrieked Doris.

The Revolt of the Miniature Mutants

"Wiktor doesn't care for us," said Ronald. "He's just using us. And you don't care for me. You keep bonking me on the head! I'm going to help these kids!"

Doris began to cuss him out. I was surprised that a hamster knew such words. Some of them even *I* had never heard before.

"Get some wire," I said to Tim. "Tie her up."

"Where am I supposed to get wire?" he asked.

"I don't know," I said in exasperation. "We're in a wall. There should be wire everywhere.

"I'll electrocute myself!"

I didn't say that this might be an improvement. After all, he *had* saved my butt while I was wrestling with Ronald.

Fortunately, Hubert came to our assistance. "Why not use her ropeline thingie?" he said.

I decided he wasn't as dumb as he sounded.

It took only a few minutes for us to get her tied up. She screamed and cussed and wiggled all the time we were doing it.

"Are you sure this will hold?" asked Tim.

"It should hold long enough," said Pleskit. "Come on, we've got to get to the gymnasium."

We could hear Doris, still cussing, as Ronald and Hubert led us toward the gym. When she fell silent, I glanced back. She was trying to bend her head forward so she could gnaw through the cords.

"Let's hurry!" I said.

As it turned out, the gym wasn't that far away — we made it in about ten minutes. But when we climbed down the wall and out through a small hole at the base of it, we faced a new problem — namely, a gym filled with sixth graders.

Do you have any idea what that looks like from a hamster's point of view? It was as if a bunch of giant oak trees had started walking around, any one of which would have squashed us flat if it had stepped on us.

Pleskit, who can do math faster in his head than most people can with a calculator, pointed out that at our size, our classmates all appeared to be well over a hundred feet tall! To get to Wiktor we were going to have to make our way through a terrifying gauntlet of death.

And even then, we had no guarantee that our tiny

The Revolt of the Miniature Mutants

ray guns could stop Wiktor before he pulled off his evil plan.

We might have hesitated, tried to plan things out a little more. But even as we stood there, Ms. Weintraub went to the microphone and said, "It is my great pleasure to present to you Ambassador Meenom Ventrah, father of our own Pleskit Meenom and first envoy to Earth from another planet."

It was certain that if the disguised Wiktor was going to go through with his plan, he would want to do it in full sight, to leave no doubt of "Meenom's" wicked action. We had no time to lose.

"Let's go!" said Pleskit.

We scurried forward, staying close to the wall when we began, since that was the safest place to be. We must have looked rather odd—three hamsters led by two ray-gun-toting, hamster-like creatures in orange uniforms.

About ten feet from the stage, the kids were packed in so tight, it no longer worked for us to hug the wall. With Pleskit leading, we began darting and dodging between people's feet. I have to say, some sixth graders have huge feet and could also stand to wash their sneakers more often. I mean, whoooiee! I climbed over one kid's feet where the smell just about knocked me out. (Turned out it was Brad. I have to talk to him about that.)

It didn't take long before one kid noticed us, of course — and as soon as that happened, she let out a scream and everyone realized we were running around loose. People were shifting, some trying to find us, some just not wanting to have a hamster run up their legs.

From my point of view, with all those feet going up and down, it looked a little like it was raining Volkswagens.

Dodging a last foot, we made it to the edge of the stage. Thank goodness for that handicapped ramp they installed a couple of years ago. I'm not sure how long it would have taken us to get up if we had had to climb the stairs.

Naturally, by this time Wiktor had realized what was going on and wanted to get rid of us. He rushed forward, murder on his face, ready to stamp and squash. I saw a huge boot come over me, and flung myself to the

side just as it smashed to the floor. But I lost my balance in doing so and couldn't move as fast as I wanted in that hamster suit. Wiktor raised his boot again.

A bloodcurdling scream split the air.

It was Rafaella, horrified at the hamster homicide about to take place. The scream threw Wiktor off, and gave me time to roll away from his boot of death.

Then Ronald pointed his ray gun at Wiktor. "Okay, Boss," he said, "that's enough!"

Wiktor stopped, a look of fury twisting his Meenom-like face.

We had him!

At least, we did until Doris came racing in from the other side of the stage. She flung herself at Ronald. At the same instant I flung myself at her.

The three of us began to wrestle.

From the corner of my beady little eye I saw Wiktor's giant hand come sweeping down to knock Ronald aside. The poor little hamster tumbled head over feet off the stage.

Everyone was screaming and hollering, trying to figure out what was going on.

I wrenched the ray gun from Doris's paws. I wanted

The Revolt of the Miniature Mutants

to enlarge myself, but I couldn't since I was the one holding the thing.

So I did the hardest thing I've ever done in my life.

I adjusted the dial on the side of the ray gun to "Enlarge."

Then I pointed it at Tim, and fired.

CHAPTER 19

[TIM]

WIKTOR NOT VICTORIOUS

When the orange ray hit me, I thought for one horrible moment that Jordan had finally crossed the line from bully to murderer.

It embarrasses me, now, to say that. But why bother with writing these things if I don't tell the truth?

I realized my mistake when I started to grow, and figured out what Jordan was hitting me with—the enlarging ray.

The feeling was both wonderful and painful—wonderful because I was glad to be getting my size back, painful both because the growing itself hurt and because the hamster suit I had on wasn't made to expand with me.

The Revolt of the Miniature Mutants

Remember, the ray wasn't really so much a growing ray as an *un*shrinking ray. But the hamster suit had never been shrunk to begin with.

So it burst apart at the seams by the time I was about ten inches high.

By the time I reached my full height, I was stark naked.

The gym rocked with a weird combination of screams and laughter—neither one of which was a very flattering reaction, if you think about it. I was embarrassed just about to death, and when I remember it now, it probably bothers me even more than the time when Mikta-makta-mookta tried to empty out the contents of our brains. But at the moment I had more important things to take care of—namely, stopping Wiktor from kidnapping Ms. Weintraub.

Roaring like a berserker, I threw myself forward and tackled Wiktor.

Of course, since he was still disguised as Meenom, everyone thought an insane naked sixth grader was attacking the alien ambassador, and the screaming got worse than ever. I could hear McNally bellowing from the far side of the gym, and I knew he was trying to push his way through the crowd.

Despite his surprise, Wiktor fought back savagely. He would have creamed me in a matter of seconds, if not for two things: One, his Meenom outfit hampered him in the same way our hamster suits had hampered us. Two, I used some of the Koo Muk Dwan techniques I had been learning from McNally.

"*Soop Yi!*" I cried, ducking and spinning, then lashing out with my foot.

Wiktor stumbled back, then lunged forward at me. I danced out of the way, laughing as I went. (This is called "the Move of the Laughing Warrior.")

This infuriated him. Taking advantage of his rage — rage adds strength but subtracts intelligence — I moved in with the Kick of the Angry Ostrich.

Wiktor went down but managed to grab my foot as he did, pulling me to the floor with him. (Remember, I hadn't been learning Koo Muk Dwan all that long!)

We struggled back and forth across the stage, where Percy had been delivering his poems not that long before. And that was the third thing that helped. Just when Wiktor almost had the best of me, I remembered a line from Percy's poem "The Rage of the Duck," the line that went, "There is no shame in defeat, only in surrender."

I wrenched myself free of Wiktor's grasp, spun him around, and locked his head in the Grip of the Disgruntled Worker.

By this time McNally had fought his way through the crowd.

"Tim, let go of the ambassador," he ordered, drawing his gun. "Drop the ambassador. I mean it, Tim. Stop this madness *now*!"

"Stand back, McNally!" I shouted. "You don't know what's going on."

"Drop him, Tim," he repeated. He sounded like he was about to cry, and I knew he was serious about shooting if I didn't let go of what seemed to be the alien ambassador.

"Look at this!" I cried.

Grabbing Wiktor by the scalp, I tried to pull off his mask.

Nothing happened!

For one, horrifying moment I was terrified that this wasn't Wiktor but the real Meenom.

"Save me, McNally!" cried Wiktor.

It was Meenom's voice. What had I done?

Then Hubert came scurrying up beside me. "Like thubbis!" he said. "Like thubbis!"

He clambered up beside me and with his tiny paws manipulated the clasp that held the mask in place.

"Now pull!" he said.

Yanking again at the fake *sphen-gnut-ksher*, I pulled off the Meenom face to reveal the evil hamster creature hidden beneath it.

CHAPTER 20

[PLESKIT]
THE FATE OF
THE HAMSTERS

I watched the battle between the evil Wiktor and the stark-naked Tim with fascinated horror. Once again I was abashed by the ability of my Earthling friend to take action. I would not like to be as warlike as the Earthlings. On the other hand, I *would* like to be able to act when it is important, rather than just standing there, foolish and useless.

On the third hand, there wasn't much I could have done in this particular case, since I was still only about four inches tall.

When Tim finally ripped Wiktor's mask from his face, a thunderous roar rose from the crowd, a weird

The Revolt of the Miniature Mutants

mixture of anger and relief and who knows what else.

McNally held Wiktor at gunpoint so Tim could let go of him.

"Someone get this kid a coat or something!" yelled my bodyguard. When no one moved fast enough, he called Ms. Weintraub over and handed her his gun, which she took with trembling hands. Then he slipped out of his own coat and passed it to Tim, who had been crouched behind the fallen Wiktor, blushing furiously.

Tim took the coat gratefully. He turned around and slipped it on. McNally is so much taller than Tim that the coat covered all those body parts that Earthlings get so weird about.

As soon as Tim was safely wrapped in McNally's coat, Rafaella rushed onto the stage and embraced him.

He turned pink all over again, though I could not tell if it was because he was pleased or embarrassed.

Meanwhile, Jordan and I had taken advantage of the confusion to scamper over against the walls, where we were safe from the huge, trampling feet of our classmates.

Hubert and Ronald came with us.

"What are we going to do?" said Jordan desperately. "I want to get back to my normal size, but I don't want to be standing here all naked!"

"You Earthlings!" I said in exasperation. "Here, make me grow."

Jordan turned the beam on me. A few moments later I had burst out of the hamster suit and was my normal size. Most people were still watching the stage; no one would have seen me at all if Tim hadn't shouted, "Hey, Pleskit!"

Then, of course, everyone turned around. I found, to my surprise and horror, that I had taken on some of the Earthling embarrassment about my body. I felt a little like I was losing my mind. I mean, what can be more natural than your own body? But, as the Fatherly One says, one always tends to pick up the attitudes of whatever culture one is living in. So I dived for my sleeping area, where I had some spare clothes. After slipping into a robe, I went to get Jordan's clothes from his sleeping area, and carried them over to him.

"Take me into the locker room," he said, sounding desperate.

I picked him up — everyone was watching me

curiously—and carried him and his clothes through the small door in the side of the gym.

A few minutes later we returned, with Jordan fully clothed.

So, he owes me big-time, as he would tend to phrase it.

About an hour after Tim had revealed Wiktor for the evil hamsteroid skeeze (Jordan's phrase) that he truly was, the real Fatherly One arrived. He was appropriately apologetic for being so late. I would have been angrier with him, but I knew he had been delayed by Wiktor's cohorts, so it was not really his fault.

Then it came down to the question of the hamsters and what to do with them.

Though they had been involved in an evil enterprise, it was only because they had been pawns of Wiktor-waktor-wooktor. Was it fair to consign them to returning to their unintelligent state?

"Oh, buh-please," said Hubert. "I *liked* being a pet. I wanna go back tuba what I was, so I can just hang out in the cage and be fed like I used to be."

Ronald, however, asked for a different fate. "I'd like

to continue my treatments," he said. "But I don't know where I can live if I do."

"You can come to the embassy," said the Fatherly One gently. He smiled and added, "It's not like you'll take up much room!"

Which left Doris.

But she had vanished in all the confusion.

Which means that somewhere in the walls of our school there lurks an evil mutant hamster woman who holds a grudge against me, my family, and my friends.

As I said, sometimes I wake up screaming.

CHAPTER 21

[PLESKIT]
A LETTER HOME

FROM: Pleskit Meenom, on the bizarre but always fascinating Planet Earth
TO: Maktel Geebrit, on the beloved and much-missed Planet Hevi-Hevi

Dear Maktel:

Well, Tim and I have survived another catastrophe. Since the Fatherly One insisted on us writing a complete report on the event, I thought I would send it on for you to see too.

As you can tell, things have not really changed since you left. My life remains one crisis after another!

I'm not sure how long I can keep this up.

As if things weren't bad enough, yesterday Tim got another interstellar postcard. The message on the back was simple, yet, in its own way, terrifying. It said: "Coming back to pick up some things I left behind." And it was signed: "Beebo."

That little guy may be one of the cutest creatures in the galaxy, but he attracts trouble the way a rotting *gishnackt* attracts *flort-burkki.*

And trouble is the last thing we need right now. Why is it that it seems impossible for us to avoid it?

Wish me luck.

Fremmix Bleeblom!

Your potentially wealthy friend,

Pleskit

A GLOSSARY OF ALIEN TERMS

Following are definitions for alien words and phrases appearing for the first time in *The Revolt of the Miniature Mutants*. The number after a definition indicates the chapter where the word first appeared.

For most words, we are only giving the spelling. In actual usage, of course, many Hevi-Hevian words would be accompanied by smells and/or body sounds.

Definitions of other extraterrestrial words appearing in this book can be found in the volumes of the Sixth-Grade Alien series where they were first used.

BEZOOTI: A wind instrument originally developed on Ffrimstan 7. The *bezooti*—also known as a "nose flute"—consists of a glass tube attached by straps and suction to the front of the face, and anywhere from seven to twenty-five "keys" used to change the tones. The number of keys depends on the number of fingers, tentacles, or other extremities possessed by the player. Fewer than twenty players have mastered the twenty-five-key *bezooti*, but their music is considered some of the most sublime ever played.

Bezooti music is known for its soothing quality — and for the oddly contrasting fact that at least three intelligent species cannot listen to it without being driven into stark raving madness. (3)

FLORT-BURKKI: Small flying insects with an annoying hum. (21)

GERTON-FARKUS: A small, furry, six-legged creature that forms pathetically intense attachments without any seeming logic. Once a *gerton-farkus* has attached itself to someone, it will follow that being everywhere, despite being yelled at, ignored, treated with contempt, or even hit. In fact, the more one tries to drive a *gerton-farkus* away, the more passionate its attachment becomes. Some people keep them as pets. Most people, however, find them disgusting. (1)

GISHNACKT: A sickeningly sweet green-and-yellow fruit harvested in the tropical regions of Hevi-Hevi. (21)

KOOBTIUK: A kind of fertilizer made from the waste products of seven different animals (including the *plonkus*), carefully balanced to provide the greatest possible blend of nutrients. While incredibly healthy for plants, the smell of *koobtiuk* is so vile that people have to have a special license and three months of training before being allowed to use it. (1)